DreamWorks

Trolls

Poppy Follows Her Nose!

Random House New York

 Published in the United States by Random House Children's Books, a division of Penguin Random House LLC, 1745 Broadway, New York, NY 10019, and in Canada by Penguin Random House Canada Limited, Toronto.
Random House and the colophon are registered trademarks of Penguin Random House LLC.
randomhousekids.com

ISBN 978-1-5247-6642-9

MANUFACTURED IN CHINA

10 9 8 7 6 5 4 3 2 1

One morning, Poppy stepped outside her pod and took a deep breath. Everything smelled like flowers, hugs, and happiness. But then she detected a whiff of something else in the air. It was the MOST DELIGHTFUL SMELL she had ever smelled!

"What is that?" Poppy asked. "I'll follow my nose and find out!"

"Hey, Poppy, check it out!" DJ Suki shouted over the music she was blasting. "I've added the sweet smell of **BERGENSCOTCH** to my beats!"

"Sounds and smells great, but I've just gotta find that smell I smell first!" Poppy called as she danced off.

"Poppy, Mr. Dinkles and I are going on a **FUZZY BEAN** picnic!" Biggie said. "Come with us!"

"I'll join you later," Poppy replied. "I'm on the hunt for the source of that *Troll*-tastic smell in the air."

"Poppy, all my new hair colors smell like COTTON CANDY," Maddy called from the door of her hair salon. "Come try one!"

"I'll be back as soon as I find that smell I smell!" Poppy promised.

"Poppy, come taste my lollipop creation," Bridget said, stopping by Troll Village for a visit. "It's my favorite, favorite, absolutely favorite vegetable in the whole world—**CANDY CORN**!"

"It smells tasty," Poppy said, "but I've just gotta find where that other smell is coming from!"

"Poppy!" cried Satin.
"Smell my new perfume—
it's LAFFODIL!"

"Now try my perfume, Poppy," Satin's twin, Chenille, said. "It's **HUG-LILY**!"

"They're both divine," Poppy told them. "But I have to keep following that smell I smell."

"Poppy, take a bite of **GLITTER–CUP**!" called Guy Diamond. "It's like a cupcake that sparkles in your mouth!"

"Mmm . . . smells good enough to eat," Poppy said. "But I've just gotta, gotta, gotta find that smell I smell."

"Poppy, help me carry this **TROLLBERRY JUICE**," Branch said. "Our friend King Gristle asked me to bring it to the clearing."

"I love Trollberry juice," Poppy said. "And that smell I've been smelling is so close. It's . . . it's—"

"PIZZA!" Poppy cheered.

"Surprise, Poppy!" King Gristle said. "I brought your favorite new snack from Bergen Town—for you and all my Troll friends!"

"Yummy!" Poppy said as she took a big sniff of the big cheese pizza . . . and then a big, big bite!